D.J.'s

FAMILY SCRAPBOOK

Devra Speregen

SCHOLASTIC INC.
New York Toronto London Auckland Sydney

ISBN 0-590-45706-3

Book designed by Ursula Herzog

12 11 10 9 8 7 6 5 4 3 2 1   2 3 4 5 6 7/9

Printed in the U.S.A.   08

First Scholastic printing, March 1992

Sometimes, life in my house can be a little nuts! We have <u>nine</u> people all living under one roof—well, ten...if you count our dog Comet. There's my dad, Danny Tanner; my two pesty little sisters, Michelle and Stephanie; my uncle Jesse and aunt Rebecca; their baby twins, Alexander and Nicholas; and my dad's oldest friend from college, Joey. And, of course, me, Donna Jo Tanner. But don't ever call me that! Everyone calls me D.J. Anyway, with so many people together, a day doesn't go by without some sort of minor catastrophe. There was even a time when things were so crazy, Stephanie drove our car right through the kitchen wall! I swear—she really did that. As for me, well, living in a full house I almost never have any privacy. But this year, I finally got my own room (Yeah!) and things are getting a little better. But you know, as bonkers as things can get around here, I wouldn't trade families with anyone else. Big families are a blast! And mine is so cool!

The other day, I found all these really neat photographs in the basement. They were just lying around, not in an album or anything, so I asked Dad if I could have them to make a Tanner family scrapbook.

He said, "Sure!" and right away he ran upstairs and went through a zillion other boxes, looking for more pictures for me to use. But that's my dad. He gets so excited about new projects—and about cleaning. He really loves to clean.

Anyway, this is my very own Tanner family scrapbook. I think it came out really cool, even though Stephanie bugged me for days to give her three more pages than anyone else (which I didn't). It's the best album. Every time I look through it, I end up laughing!

Me, D.J. (Donna Jo) Tanner

How embarrassing! I can't believe Dad kept this dorky picture of me from when I was eleven. I hate that dumb space between my teeth!

Here I am at thirteen. Seventh grade was so cool. That was the first year I worked on the school newspaper.

I like this picture that dad took of me last year. I look so grown-up and mature, even though I was still in junior high school. Boy, was last year crazy! So many things happened in our family: Uncle Jesse got married, Stephanie got on the <u>boy's</u> Little League, Michelle went to preschool, and Joey was on <u>Star Search</u>.

This is me now—a high school girl! High school is the ultimate! And now I have my own room <u>and</u> a driver's license learning permit! If I can only convince Dad to get me my own car....

Stephanie Tanner

If I had to describe my sister in one word, I would say "tomboy." But then again, she is very feminine. Steph even takes dancing lessons. Still she's so good at sports. That's how come she made the boy's Little League last year! I personally don't know what she sees in all that sports stuff—except maybe that it sure is a great way to meet guys!

Steph is 5 years younger than me, and is usually a royal pain. But I have to admit, she is pretty cool—in her own annoying way. I think she's really funny, too...for a kid, anyway. Although she may be a pain, she knows how to keep a secret.

Well, sometimes I have to <u>help</u> her keep a secret!

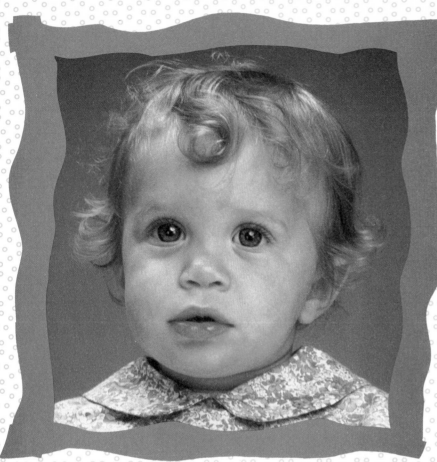

Michelle
Tanner

People tell me I have the cutest little sisters. Steph is cute, of course, but Michelle is a whole other story. She is totally adorable! Since she was born, everyone just <u>oohs</u> and <u>ahhs</u> over her. And don't think they've stopped just because she's in kindergarten now. In fact, they <u>ooh</u> and <u>aah</u> even more!

Michelle likes to copy me and Stephanie all the time. She says whatever we say— even though she probably has no idea what it means! I remember when this picture was taken. It was when Michelle and Uncle Jesse went shopping together. Here's Michelle copying Uncle Jesse!

Michelle's favorite expressions are: "This is nuts!" and "Watch it, Mister!"

She's only five, but boy, what a ham!!!

Danny Tanner

My dad is the coolest. He's never mean, and he always listens to what we kids have to say. Since my mother died, he's had to be both parents to me and my sisters. I think he's done a really good job at it, too. Kimmy says dad is weird because he irons his socks. But Dad isn't weird—he's just abnormally neat! In fact, my dad is probably the most organized man in San Francisco. Not only does he iron socks, he hangs bow ties, and he waxes the floor in our attic!

Dad is a talk show host on a regular day-time network program. He works very long hours at the TV station, but he always makes time for Michelle, Steph, and me.

Last year, during the public television an-
nual telethon, Dad was the host...and he
fell asleep on the air! He doesn't know
that Uncle Jesse took this picture of him
fast asleep while the cameras were still
rolling! Wait till he sees this!

Here's Dad trying to be cool
like Uncle Jesse!

Did I tell you how funny my dad is? He's
a real joker. Maybe not as funny as Joey,
but he really makes me laugh. Here he is
at our gym, pretending to lift weights.
Nice try, Dad!

Uncle Jesse Katsopolis

This is Uncle Jesse when he first came to live with us five years ago. Obviously, he was having a "Bad Hair Day"! (Just kidding, Uncle Jesse!)

This is him now. No wonder all my girlfriends always drool over him!

Uncle Jesse is a real rocker. He's the greatest musician and songwriter I know. This year, his dreams are finally coming true—he's signed a recording contract! Won't it be awesome when Jesse and the Rippers become as famous as R.E.M.?

This was the time when Uncle Jesse played guitar for Michelle's nursery school class. He'd do anything for us girls—that's just the kind of guy he is.

Uncle Jesse is <u>always</u> goofing around. I think he likes to pretend he's someone famous. I always catch him in front of the mirror, pretending he's Elvis Presley or Sammy Davis, Jr.!

Joey Gladstone

Joey is the funniest guy in the entire world. He makes us laugh until our stomachs hurt! Before he came to live with us, he used to be a stand-up comedian. Then, last year, he won a spot on <u>Star Search</u>!

This year, Joey landed the most perfect job. He hosts a Saturday morning cartoon show. It's perfect for him because he's the best cartoon voice impersonator. You should hear him do Popeye and Bullwinkle!

Joey always tries to make us laugh when we're sad. Here he is trying to cheer up Steph at her Honey Bee slumber party. Rebecca was supposed to take Steph to the Honey Bee's mother-and-daughter sleepover, but her car broke down and she couldn't make it. Joey came to the rescue—wearing his Teenage Mutant Ninja Turtle pajamas—and made everyone laugh!

Sometimes, Joey's sense of humor gets him in trouble. Once, when we were at the gym, he made fun of a big weightlifter guy. That guy could have squashed him like a bug, but luckily, Joey can talk himself out of anything!

When Joey first came to live with us, he was nervous about fitting in. Today, he is one of the family!

Rebecca
Donaldson-Katsopolis

This is Aunt Rebecca. She and Jesse got married last year in a beautiful church with a choir and everything. They almost missed their wedding when Uncle Jesse decided to try a parachute jump from an airplane, and they had to grab a passing bus to the church! Becky was wearing her wedding gown! Luckily, they made it on time, and had the most beautiful wedding ever. I was a bridesmaid and so was Stephanie. Michelle was the cutest flower girl!

Before they got married, this is how Uncle Jesse wanted to look for his wedding—him as Elvis and Becky as Priscilla. I don't know about him sometimes....I mean, does he really think he's Elvis? Aunt Becky, on the other hand, told me she always dreamed of getting married in her home-town in Nebraska. I guess they both compromised...but I'll bet they're both glad they did!

Uncle Jesse read in some book that when you play music to babies before they're born, they can hear it. It was so funny when he put the Walkman on Aunt Rebecca's stomach! He played an Elvis tape, of course!

Don't they make the cutest couple?

Aunt Becky and Uncle Jesse were sure surprised to find out they were having a baby...but not as surprised as when they found out that they were having twins! Uncle Jesse carried around an X-ray picture (or whatever they call it) of Nicholas and Alex for weeks. What a proud daddy!

Memorable Moments

New Year's Eve is the only night Michelle (and Comet!) get to stay up past 9:30! I took this picture with the camera Dad gave me for Christmas. Don't they look cute?

I can't believe I found this picture! When Uncle Jesse and Joey moved in, we used to picnic in the park all the time. This was the day that Dad begged us to take a nice family picture of a day at the park. But when we asked this guy off the street to take the picture, Joey put the funny glasses on Michelle and we were laughing too hard to take a serious picture. The guy thought we were nuts!

Every year at Christmas, Daddy makes us pose for these geeky family photos. Then, he has them blown up into portrait size. It wouldn't be so bad, except for the fact that he insists on showing <u>all</u> of them when I bring a date to the house! Do you think I want my dates to see me looking like El Dorko?

Anyway, last year I actually liked our Tanner family Christmas photo. I even let Dad show it to my junior prom date.

My Teen Times

This was my very first year as a "teen"! Dad made me a great party on my thirteenth birthday.

This was when Dad refused to buy me a pair of Blow Out sneakers so I got a job at a photo studio to earn enough money to buy them myself. I know I look pretty dorky, but I got paid to look dorky! Here I am trying to make this grumpy little brat smile for a professional photographer. We only have this picture because Dad came down to the mall where I worked to spy on me!

This is Kimmy Gibler. We've been best friends practically forever. She lives down the block, but everyone thinks she hangs around our house more than her own. I took this picture on our first day of high school.

Dad, Jesse, and Joey

I don't think there are three guys in this whole world that are cooler than my dad, my uncle Jesse, and Joey.

For a couple of years, Uncle Jesse and Joey ran their own company. They started up a TV commercial jingle-writing company, and they wrote some pretty awesome jingles.

Here they are practicing a pitch to land a big ad account. (Joey taught me all that cool advertising lingo!)

Now Uncle Jesse is a big-time rocker! He says that little Michelle sometimes gives him inspiration when he's writing songs.

Joey says his new job is really cool. He's always dreamed about working with Toons! Now, he says, he's a professional Toon! Here he is doing impressions.

Adorable Michelle Moments

I still can't believe it, but there is a little cousin of ours from Greece who looks <u>exactly</u> like Michelle—but with black hair! When Uncle Jesse's grandparents came to visit last year, they bought little Malina with them. Isn't the resemblance remarkable?

Here's Michelle looking very nervous on her first day of kindergarten!

It was so funny when Uncle Jesse went clothes shopping for Michelle. She looks like one tough little cookie!

Sometimes Comet tries to sneak into Michelle's bed to sleep. Dad says it was cute when he was a little puppy, but that now Comet should sleep in his own bed. (Dad doesn't know that Stephanie and I take turns letting Comet sleep with us!)

Michelle loves to work out at the junior gym. She can even do a cartwheel!

Silly Stephanie Moments

I think this was probably Stephanie's worst day ever. Can you believe she actually drove our car through the kitchen? I didn't think anyone would believe me, that's why I took this picture. Dad said he could use it for insurance purposes, too. Steph was real sorry—I mean, it was an accident and all. She's happy we have an understanding Dad.

This was the day that Stephanie got glasses. She doesn't look that bad, but of course I like to blackmail her with this picture!

More
Memorable
Moments

When Michelle was a baby, I remember
how it took Uncle Jesse and Joey all day
to learn how to change her diaper!

Oh, this picture makes me cry! Remember when Comet had puppies? Look how cute they are! I wish we could have kept them all.

I took this picture on the very first night that Joey and Uncle Jesse came to live with us. Boy, have we all changed!

This was when Uncle Jesse invited the Beach Boys to our house! I was the coolest kid at school for a whole week when the kids found out that I knew the Beach Boys!

Here's Joey on <u>Star Search</u>!

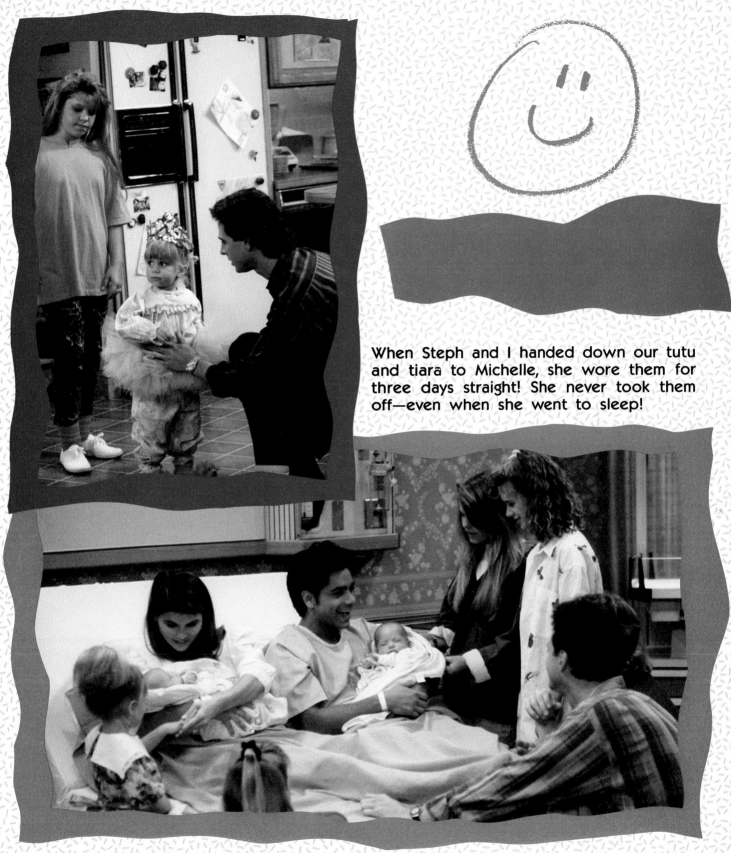

When Steph and I handed down our tutu and tiara to Michelle, she wore them for three days straight! She never took them off—even when she went to sleep!

Joey took this picture of us visiting Aunt Rebecca and Uncle Jesse at the hospital after the twins were born. Aren't Nicholas and Alex the sweetest babies?

Sisterly Love

This is my favorite picture of me and my sisters. I think we look alike. Everyone tells me I look like Mom. When our mom died, I was young, but Stephanie was really little. Sometimes it's hard on us, not having a mother, but we help each other through those rough times. They're pests, but most of the time it's great to have sisters.

Stephanie is the most outgoing sister of all of us. I think she's also the strangest.

Here's Stephanie taking Michelle to her first day of kindergarten. Michelle was so scared! Stephanie must have told her about <u>her</u> first day, and how Dad watched her through the window for <u>three</u> hours until the teacher asked him to leave!

When Kimmy and I try to have a little privacy, pesky Steph always wants to be included.

If she doesn't get rid of that annoying recorder, I'm going to lose my mind!

Here we are again, officially handing down the Tanner girls tutu and tiara to Michelle.

My Personal Stuff

Last year I got really sick when I went on sort of a crash diet. Kimmy was having a pool party and I didn't want to wear a bathing suit until I lost weight. Boy, was that stupid. What happened was I really overdid it at the health club, and I hadn't eaten in two days. Luckily, Dad set me straight, and Aunt Rebecca taught me how to eat better.

I sure do remember this day. It was when I got an F on my science test and didn't tell Dad. I finally did come clean and tell him. It's a darn good thing I have such a cool, understanding Dad. (Now can I get a car, Dad?)

Family Snapshots

Here we are: The entire Tanner clan and company through the years!

D.J. Tanner

Joey Gladstone

Jesse Katsopoulis

Rebecca Katsopoulis

Stephanie Tanner

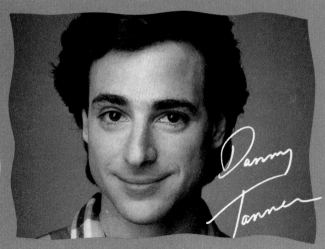

Danny Tanner

MICHELLE TANNER